THE LOST
WORLD

HellioN
THE FIERY
FOE

D0193467

With special thanks to Lucy Courtenay

For Tilly because girls like Beasts too

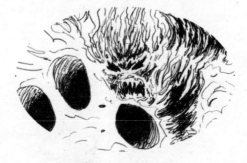

www.beastquest.co.uk

ORCHARD BOOKS
338 Euston Road, London NW1 3BH
Orchard Books Australia
Level 17/207 Kent St, Sydney, NSW 2000

A Paperback Original
First published in Great Britain in 2010

Beast Quest is a registered trademark of Working Partners Limited
Series created by Beast Quest Limited, London

Text © Beast Quest Limited 2010
Cover illustration by Steve Sims © Orchard Books 2010
Inside illustrations by Ovi@kja-artists.com © Orchard Books 2010

A CIP catalogue record for this book is available from
the British Library.

ISBN 978 1 40830 730 4

7 9 10 8

Printed and bound by CPI Group (UK) Ltd, Croydon, CR0 4YY

The paper and board used in this paperback are natural recyclable
products made from wood grown in sustainable forests. The
manufacturing processes conform to the environmental regulations of
the country of origin.

Orchard Books is a division of Hachette Children's Books,
an Hachette UK company

www.hachette.co.uk

HELLION
THE FIERY
FOE

BY ADAM BLADE

ORCHARD

THE FOREST
OF DOOM

SOUTHERN RIVER

THE
SCARLET
DESERT

Welcome to another world, where Dark Forces are at play.

Tom thought he was on his way back home; he was wrong. My son has entered another realm where nothing is as it seems. Six monstrous Beasts threaten all corners of the kingdom, and Tom and Elenna must face an enemy they thought long gone. I have never been so proud of my son, but can he be all that I always hoped he would be? Or shall a mother watch her son fail?

One question remains. Are you brave enough to join Tom on the most deadly Quest yet?

Only you know the answer...

Freya, Mistress of the Beasts

PROLOGUE

Eldor lifted his head and sniffed the air, feeling the breeze tickle his vast antlers. The stag smelt nothing unusual in his forest kingdom. His does were safe as they grazed, with their fawns close by. And yet...

Eldor had long been king of this forest. It held no secrets for him. His senses were as sharp as an eagle's talons, and had never once let him down. And now they were telling him that a change was in the air.

And, in the forest, change was never good.

Eldor leant his head back and roared a warning to the unseen enemy. The does looked up, flicking their ears in alarm. Fawns sensed their mothers' unease and pressed closer, their soft speckled bodies trembling. Eldor walked slowly in the midst of his family, looking for unfamiliar tracks on the forest floor.

Eldor's head darted up. His nostrils flared. His body tensed. On the air was the scent of the thing he and his family most feared.

Smoke.

Eldor would never forget the day when, as a fawn, fire had ravaged the woods. His father had perished, as had many others – of all clans and species. Eldor's nerves quivered as a rabbit darted between his legs with wide fearful eyes. In the distance, a curl of smoke twisted among the trees.

The does and fawns clustered together, moving uncertainly from side to side, judging which way to run. With twittering terror, birds dived through the air above their heads. The ground was alive with movement. Mice, weasels, rabbits, foxes, voles. All the creatures of the forest were fleeing.

Eldor brought his panic under control, bellowing a warning to his herd. The does and fawns scattered, heading for the edge of the forest and the open ground beyond. They might be exposed to predators out of the trees, but at least there they could outrun the fire.

As a path of orange widened before him, Eldor stood his ground, making sure that all his family had a headstart. A huge rolling fireball was racing through the undergrowth now, the heat from it making Eldor's eyes sting. Too late, he realised it was picking up speed. It seemed to change course at will, as though alive, heading straight towards him. With a mighty bound, he leapt out of the way and landed beside a pile of dry leaves. A stray spark from the fireball touched them and they caught fire as Eldor skittered to a stop. He stamped the flames out with his hooves.

This was no ordinary fire. Eldor sensed a heart and a mind behind the savage heat. As the stag watched, the ball changed shape – limbs seemed to

reach out of a torso that lengthened
and grew. The fire was transformed
into a giant man-shaped monster
with skin of flaming orange. Eyes of
flickering fire blazed in its face. Its
burning arms tapered away into
fingers trailing black tendrils of

smoke. Eldor felt a wave of relief that his family and the other woodland creatures had already made their escape. He knew that he might die here this day, but he would not slink away like a coward.

The fiery horror loomed as high as the trees. The smoke was choking, and scorched his throat. It was almost impossible to see. Eldor lunged blindly towards his foe. He did not know how he was going to combat this terror, but his instinct drove him forward. This Beast had to be stopped.

As he passed straight through the attacker's body, Eldor cried out in agony. He smelt the bitter stench of his own singed fur. Glancing round to inspect his body, he saw the raw, charred flesh of a burn wound in his flank. Eldor staggered, almost overwhelmed by pain that felt like it would consume him whole.

The man of fire sent out a dart of flame. It hit the ground with deadly force, throwing up sparks. Eldor reared up on his hind legs, then lunged at the Beast with his antlers. Eldor's enemy howled in fury as the antlers connected with the living creature behind the fire. The Beast took a backward step, flaming arms raised menacingly.

Eldor shook his antlers free of lingering flames and readied himself for another attack on the Beast. He could not back down.

Something evil had come to his forest. Eldor would defeat it, or die trying.

CHAPTER ONE

A TWISTED KINGDOM

Tom patted Storm's flank and took one last look over his shoulder at the oasis, where dozens of villagers were gathered at the water's edge. Now Convol was defeated, the great lizard wouldn't terrorise their oasis any more. They wouldn't go thirsty again. Others were already carrying full buckets back to their village.

Beyond the water, the Scarlet Desert stretched as far as the horizon.

It's as if I'm looking at the Ruby Desert back home, he thought.

This strange kingdom of Tavania was almost identical to Avantia. But it was also full of nasty surprises. King Hugo didn't sit on the throne here. Instead, the Evil Wizard Malvel ruled.

They had met a fat and friendly prison guard called Dalaton on their first adventure in Tavania. Freya, Tom's mother, believed she could train him to be the land's Master of the Beasts.

The Beasts that were destroying this kingdom were not evil, like so many of the magical creatures Tom had faced. They had been torn from their natural homes and brought to

Tavania through strange portals in the sky. Lost and confused, they struggled to control their immense power and were seriously damaging Tavania. Tom and Elenna had already helped one Beast, Convol, get back to where he belonged, closing one of the six deadly portals.

Now, a new Beast awaited.

"A Beast of fire and rage," said Elenna as she walked beside Storm. Silver, Elenna's wolf, padded beside her. "I wonder what Oradu meant by that?"

"I don't know," said Tom. "But we'll find out soon enough."

Oradu was Tavania's Good Wizard, and he was their only guide here. Malvel had robbed him of his powers by taking his six magical tokens and leaving him almost powerless, forcing him to flee the kingdom. But with each Beast Tom and Elenna defeated, Oradu's power grew. They already had his wizard's robe, which was stored safely in Storm's saddlebag.

Tom climbed into the saddle and Elenna hoisted herself up behind him. He clicked his tongue, and Storm broke into a trot. The village was in sight now. Villagers were gathered around their houses, cheering.

Smiling and nodding at the villagers as they clustered around, Tom sought the figure of the boy who had lent cloaks to him and Elenna. Storm whinnied in recognition as the boy pushed through the crowd towards them.

"You saved us," he said, smiling broadly. "Thank you!"

"You saved us, too," Tom grinned, handing back the cloaks. "Without these we'd have been scorched out there in the heat."

"Good luck to you," said the boy, disappearing back into the crowd.

Elenna pushed her dark hair away from her eyes. "Where do we find the next Beast?" she asked Tom.

"Perhaps Oradu's map will show us," said Tom.

Reaching into the saddlebag, Elenna drew out a thick square of hinged gold. She opened it up, and pushed the clasp until the map of Tavania shimmered before them. Tom found it odd to stare at a place that was so familiar – and yet so strange at the same time.

"We have to go here," he said, pointing at what looked like a miniature rip in the air above the centre of the map. He looked closely at the pattern etched onto the golden map. Clustered below the portal was a stand of small trees. Tiny letters appeared beside it.

"The Forest of Doom," Elenna read. Her eyes widened. "It's exactly where the Forest of Fear is back home!"

"It will seem the same, but we must be on our guard," Tom said as he folded up the map again. "The trees themselves might be on Malvel's side." Tom shuddered as he remembered how he and Elenna had almost been drowned by a river that had come alive as they tried to take a drink. Here in Tavania, nature itself seemed to do the Dark Wizard's bidding.

Silver threw back his shaggy head and howled. The air seemed to swallow up the sound.

Perhaps Malvel is watching us even now, Tom thought.

They said goodbye to the grateful villagers. With Elenna sitting behind him, Tom nudged Storm into a canter, heading north.

"I won't miss the heat of the desert," said Elenna.

"Me neither," said Tom, turning his face into the cooling wind.

The land grew greener as they moved further away from the desert, towards the mountains and the Forest of Doom. They made good progress. It wasn't long before the Scarlet Desert was little more than a shimmer behind them.

But Tom couldn't relax. From the saddle, he gazed around. He didn't trust this place. It seemed strange that they hadn't passed anyone. *Perhaps the road that we're on is moving, leading us back the way we've come?*

Silver also seemed wary. His ears were pricked, and the hackles on his back rose as he whined uneasily.

"Hush," Elenna soothed. "Everything is fine."

The road was moving steadily uphill. There were rolling foothills now, growing steeper with every turn. Soon, soft green gave way to hard grey stone. The mountains loomed over them, grave and dark.

Tom's stomach rumbled. He realised they hadn't stopped to eat since leaving the Scarlet Desert. Glancing around did nothing to cheer his spirits. Nothing grew here, so high up in the mountains. Cursing himself for not taking more care, Tom pressed on.

Storm stopped so suddenly that Tom almost tumbled out of the saddle. Tom tapped the stallion's flanks with his heels to encourage him onwards. Storm refused to move. Despite Elenna's soothing words, Silver began pacing back and forth. Then he howled, the echo of it shaking the mountain walls.

Tom tensed. There was nobody on the road ahead of them, and nobody behind. The mountainsides were bare and bleak. They were completely alone. So what was frightening the animals?

"What is happening?" asked Elenna, her voice quivering.

"I don't—" Tom began.

He was interrupted by the low, deep sound of stone shifting over stone. Tom felt Elenna clutch at him as Storm reared in terror.

The mountain was moving!

The terrible moaning sound of grating stone boomed around them. Pillars of rock rose up out of the

mountain path to form a solid wall,
blocking their way.

The land of Tavania was turning on
them once again!

CHAPTER TWO

THE GRANITE MAZE

The rocks grew upwards like grotesque granite trees. Storm bucked, and Tom fought to stay in the saddle. Silver ran at the growing stones, growling ferociously.

"We have to turn back!" Elenna shouted over the noise.

"No!" Tom yelled back as he struggled to keep his stallion steady.

More pillars were sprouting around them, forming a corridor of stone. "That's what Malvel wants. We must reach the Forest of Doom!"

He dug his heels into Storm's sides and raced towards a gap in the stone. A chance of escape! But as Storm reached the gap, Tom saw more of the same greyness beyond, looping around them like a knot. The sound was unbearable and Tom was beginning to feel disorientated.

As the last of the gloomy shadows from the columns fell over them, the terrible grinding ceased. The silence felt heavy as Tom looked over his shoulder to see that new columns had formed – they were blocked off in all directions.

It's a maze, Tom realised. *Malvel's latest obstacle.*

Silver bounded towards one of the pillars. His paws scrabbled on the smooth stone surface, and he fell back with a growl.

Elenna slid off Storm's back and sank to the ground with her head in her hands. "This is too much," she muttered. "We're trapped here."

Tom gritted his teeth. "We found our way out of that maze in our fight to rescue Vedra and Krimon," he said. "Do you remember that? We can do this."

Carefully, Tom took his feet out of Storm's stirrups.

"What are you doing?" Elenna asked, looking up.

"If I stand on Storm's back," Tom said, "I might just be able to see over the pillars."

Elenna's eyes flared with hope.

"Whoa boy," Elenna soothed the uneasy stallion as Tom stood up. He wobbled once, then righted himself. He stretched up as high as he dared.

"I can see over them!" he called down. "You lead Storm, Elenna, and I'll guide us out. But go slow – I need to keep my balance."

Elenna walked slowly with Silver beside her, holding Storm's bridle and calming the stallion with gentle words. Tom concentrated on keeping his balance, spreading his arms out to the sides. He craned his neck to peer over the columns. He could see dark, jagged lines where corridors cut through the solid grey stones. Twisting one way, turning another.

"Left!" he called, thinking he had figured the way out.

Storm stumbled. Tom dropped to his knees, landing hard in the saddle. *Let's try that again*, he thought. He stood up straight and gazed across the top of the maze. "Now right!" he said. "Straight on, Elenna...good boy, Storm...right again!"

They made slow progress as they moved deeper into the rocky labyrinth.

"I can see the end," Tom said at last. "Just two more turns!"

The gloom of the maze began to ease. Tom slid back into Storm's saddle. He followed the strip of sunlight guiding them towards the way out.

"We made it!"

Elenna whooped as they stepped

out into the brightness of the day once again.

Tom closed his eyes and tipped his face up to the sky. Storm whinnied in triumph.

They had emerged onto a broad green plateau. Shrubs, plants and grass grew all around. As he dismounted to help Elenna hunt for food, Tom breathed a sigh of relief. He had overcome Malvel's first test, but he knew worse – much worse – still awaited.

"A yucca!" Elenna pounced on a familiar, spiky-leaved plant. "And I can see fruit, Tom!"

"Watch out for the leaves," Tom warned. "They're as sharp as blades."

Elenna carefully reached among the leaves and plucked the fresh green fruit.

The colour returned to Elenna's cheeks as they sat side-by-side, eating the fruit. It was a little bland, but it filled their stomachs and quenched their thirst. Storm cropped the grass quietly, while Silver lapped at a nearby puddle of rainwater that had collected in the hollow of a rock.

"Look at the way the sunlight bounces off the sky here," Elenna said. "Isn't it strange?"

Tom looked up. The dark portal

pulsed over their heads, and clouds reflected in the sky's surface, making it seem glassier than ever. Being in Tavania felt like being in a great, glass dome.

"Time to move on," he said.

He leapt into the saddle as Elenna called to Silver. They set off again, following the golden map. Tom couldn't shake off the feeling of being enclosed – trapped. But they had to keep going.

Tavania needed them.

CHAPTER THREE

THE FOREST OF DOOM

Tom felt a chill run down his spine when he saw the dark shadow of the Forest of Doom lurking on the horizon. He guided Storm onwards. There was no turning back. The Beast awaited.

The landscape had grown steadily greener again since Tom and Elenna had left the mountains behind.

The trees were changing, too, from dark mountain pines to the grassy colours of beech and oak.

"Something is glimmering up ahead," Elenna said, pointing over Tom's shoulder down the road. "Is it water?"

Tom checked the golden map. "There's a lake beside the forest, look," he said, and showed Elenna. Squinting into the sun, he could make out the dark-blue edges of the lake shore that fringed the Forest of Doom. He hoped they might be able to fill their flasks at the lake's edge.

Silver started howling. Tom followed the wolf's gaze to the trees – emerging from them was a family of three wolf cubs, their thick silvery coats fuzzy and soft. Now they were tumbling down a steep bank which

ran from the edge of the forest.

"Look at the little wolves playing, Tom!" Elenna smiled, as Silver raced towards them.

Tom frowned. It didn't look like a game to him. The cubs were sliding down the hill too fast, tumbling over each other and scrabbling to grip the hillside. At the top of the slope, their mother appeared, pacing back and forth.

Tom started forward. "I think they're in trouble!" he said.

Silver was already at the foot of the hill, poised and alert. As the cubs barrelled towards him, he turned to stop them gently against his flank. The cubs leapt and fawned around him. Silver butted them firmly with his snout, back up the hill to where their mother was waiting anxiously. As the cubs scrambled back up to cluster around their mother, she howled at the sky.

Tom felt Elenna tense behind him. "What's happ—"

Her words died at what they saw next. All around them, animals seemed to be fleeing the forest. A family of foxes darted past with their tails following them like smoke; squirrels crisscrossed between Storm's legs, far from their homes; birds flapped and squawked overhead. Tom's guts tingled with unease – something was making the wildlife leave the safety of the forest.

They dismounted and moved cautiously onwards, past the dark lake towards the trees. Storm whinnied softly, and Silver began to whine. There was a fluttering sound close by. A bird was struggling feebly in the earth at the foot of a dark oak tree.

"Poor thing," Elenna gasped. "It must have fallen out of its nest."

Tom crouched to gently scoop up the bird. The tiny bundle of feathers shivered in his hands. The edges of its wings were brown and singed. He looked up to the oak tree – there was no nest, only bare branches.

"This bird didn't fall out of any nest," Tom said. "Its wings are burnt, and there's no sign of fire here. It must have fallen as it flew from somewhere else."

Silver sniffed the bird, but drew back at the burnt smell on its feathers.

Tucking the bird carefully into his tunic, Tom seized the lowest branch of the oak tree, swinging himself upwards. From there he could see smoke drifting faintly over the treetops. Armed with this fresh knowledge, he laid the bird carefully in the crook of a branch and climbed back down.

"There's a fire, deep inside the forest," he said, as he rejoined Elenna. "That's why the animals are leaving. It can only be the Beast."

They gazed at the dark spread of the forest ahead. A rabbit broke cover, bounding towards them. Storm shied to the side. Tom fought to bring the stallion back under control, wrestling with the reins while keeping his feet planted on the ground.

"That rabbit's tail was almost burnt away," he said, twisting round to watch the little animal dart off. "The Beast is attacking the animals that live here. It must be mad with rage – away from its natural home, wherever that may be. Just like Convol."

Elenna shivered. "'A Beast of fire and rage'," she whispered.

As Elenna spoke, a stag plunged out of the trees. Its eyes were wild. Foam sprayed from its mouth and its

sides were dark with sweat. It was
heading straight towards them.

"Get out of the way, Elenna!" Tom
shouted.

Elenna grasped Silver by the scruff
of the neck and threw herself to the
side as the stag bore down on them.
Tom tugged on Storm's bridle to
pull the stallion to safety, but he

overbalanced and lost his grip, stumbling to the ground directly in the path of the stag's hooves.

Eyes rolling, the stag raced towards him. Tom could see a nasty burn on its side. The creature's eyes looked delirious with pain. Tom threw himself against a tree as it raced past. The creature turned and stared at him, snorting angrily. It lowered its antlers and charged. Tom knew he would either be trampled or skewered against the tree.

There was no escape.

CHAPTER FOUR

DESPERATE MEASURES

Tom curled himself into a ball, hearing a jarring thud behind him as the stag's antlers thudded into the tree-trunk. Rolling, Tom missed the animal's trampling hooves by a hair's breadth. But, just as he tried to right himself, Tom felt the ground dip beneath him, and his rolling picked up pace.

He'd hit a slope!

As he rolled over and over, Tom spread his arms to dig his fingers into the dirt, stopping his own momentum. As he pulled himself to his feet, he saw the stag still standing by the tree. It seemed dazed, uncertain what to do next. Then it swung its head from side to side, searching, snorting with growing rage. When its black eyes found Tom, it charged down the slope.

Silver darted into the stag's path like a streak of smoke, nipping at the stag's ankles. Undeterred, the stag raced on towards Tom, leaving Silver behind. Elenna fitted an arrow to her bow and let it fly. The arrow pierced the ground before the stag. The stag faltered and stopped, taking a few backward steps.

"Again!" Tom called, realising

Elenna's accuracy could scare the stag away.

Elenna's second arrow joined the first, quivering in the ground with its feathers waving. The stag tossed its mighty head and bellowed again. Turning at last, it crashed away through the undergrowth – and vanished from sight.

Breathing more easily, Tom looked round for Storm. His stallion picked his way down the slope towards him, stopping with his head low and reins dangling.

"Easy," Tom said, stroking Storm's neck. "You're safe. He won't be coming back."

The lake bordering the Forest of Doom was only a short distance away. Tom walked to the shore, holding Storm lightly by the reins. The stallion dipped his head into the dark water and drank deeply.

"Did you see the burn on that stag's side?" Elenna said as she and Silver joined them. "The poor creature was mad with pain."

Tom nodded. "We must find the Beast who is causing this fire," he said. "And we have to send him home."

Elenna grew pale. "I can't fight

fire," she whispered.

Tom felt a jolt as he remembered:
when she was a baby, Elenna had
lost her parents in a terrible fire. She
had almost lost her own life, too.

He put his hand on his friend's
shoulder. "That fire was a long
time ago."

Elenna shook her head. Tom could
see she was trembling. "They couldn't
get out," she whispered. Tom knew
she was talking about her parents.
"I dream about them sometimes."

Tom gazed around for inspiration.
How could he reassure Elenna that
everything would be all right?

He caught the inviting gleam of
the lake. The water looked fresh
and cool.

"Perhaps we should soak our
clothes?" he said. "Fire can't burn

us if we're soaking wet."

Elenna gazed at the lake. Tom felt her trembling ease as she took a shaky breath. "Good idea," she said, nodding.

Before Tom could react, her palm was thrust into his chest. Tom's arms waved as he toppled backwards with a splash. The cool lake water enveloped him. When he broke the surface again, he heard Elenna's laughter singing through the forest. Tom spat out some water as he reached up to grab Elenna's sleeve, pulling her into the water with him.

"Why...you..." she gasped as she resurfaced.

Tom grinned, flicking water into her eyes. "It seemed fair," he said.

Laughing, Elenna splashed him back. Tom ducked down under the

water, enjoying the silky chill of the
lake as it bathed the bumps and
bruises of his close encounter with
the stag. Elenna swam down like an
otter beside him, her dark hair
fanning out like water-weed.

Coming up for air, Tom and Elenna
played in the water for a while
longer. Storm and Silver watched
from the bank. After a few minutes,
Tom climbed out of the water and
walked up the sandy shore to take
Storm's bridle.

"In you come, boy," he coaxed,
backing towards the lake again.

"A nice wet coat will keep you safe, as well."

With a snort, Storm tugged his bridle from Tom's hands and trotted away from the water. Elenna had no luck with Silver either. It was clear that their companions wanted nothing more from the lake than a long, cool drink.

Tom's laughter died. He wasn't here for fun and games.

A few moments later, Tom and Elenna stepped cautiously into the Forest of Doom. Their clothes were still soaked and dripped water onto the dry ground. Storm and Silver walked beside them, their ears pricked and alert.

Snaking fingers of smoke crept among the trees. The way it broke apart and then reformed to drift across their path was eerie. It was as if the smoke itself was alive. The smell of burning was strong, making Tom's eyes water. He could hear Elenna shivering on the other side of Storm, her bow gripped tight in her hands. He knew how hard this was for her.

"We'll follow that," Tom said, pointing at the smoke.

The scent of destruction and fear was all around them. As they walked, they passed the cinder skeletons of trees burnt clean of leaves, finding patches of dry ground where tiny flames still flickered. Birds lay dead on the ground. Huge flakes of ash were scattered across blackened branches like grey petals.

Covering their mouths from the choking smoke as best they could,

Tom and Elenna picked their way among the tree roots that rose from the ground like serpents. Fallen trees and hanging vines that had survived the flames made progress difficult. Storm stumbled as his hoof caught in a burnt tangle of brambles.

Tom swiped at the vines. "We need to find a clearer way through the trees to reach the heart of this place," he said.

But there were no easy paths. As they struggled on, doubling back time and again as the going grew too difficult, one thing became clear. Even amid its terrible destruction, the Forest of Doom was turning on them, trying to stop their Quest.

A thorny bramble lashed at his cheek. "I've never encountered such a hostile place," he said wearily.

"How can we fight a whole kingdom, Elenna?"

"We need to stay brave and strong," Elenna replied. "Remember, Malvel is counting on us losing heart. We can't let him win."

Tom could only imagine how hard it was for Elenna to stay calm in the face of her greatest fear. He felt ashamed – if she could be brave, so could he. As he pushed past the grasping vines, he pulled out the rusty, heavy sword that he had borrowed from the Tavanian palace. He hacked at the vegetation. It was not much of a weapon, but it was the best he had. His own sword and shield had been stolen by Malvel.

Finally Tom heard the sound that he had been dreading.

The crackle of flames.

CHAPTER FIVE

BALLS OF FLAME

The smoke around them thickened.
Tom coughed violently, his eyes
streaming tears that he wiped
away to peer through the swirling
ash cloud.

In the distant depths of the forest,
he saw an orange blur pass between
the trees. It trailed fire like a comet.

"What was that?" whispered
Elenna.

Tom's grip tightened on his sword. He saw it again – closer. The shape was a ball of fire, rolling across the ground. Everything it touched burst into flame. Trees collapsed like skittles. Burning branches crashed to the ground. Leaves went up in flashes of orange and gold. It had to be the Beast!

Storm whinnied and reared up on his hind legs, his eyes rolling back, white and panicked. Silver growled, pacing back and forth, determined not to leave Elenna's side but clearly terrified of the intense heat. Tom could hear Elenna's ragged breathing as she stared at her very worst nightmare come true.

He gazed around desperately, trying to blink away the tears in his smoke-filled eyes. Everywhere was burnt and black. At last he saw a vast redwood tree, standing alone in a nearby clearing. There was a deep hole in the base of its trunk, large enough to hold Storm and Silver.

"There!" he shouted over the noise of burning.

They coaxed Silver and Storm towards the redwood. Tom gazed up at the towering tree with its distinctive red bark. He'd never seen anything so large. Why hadn't it burned?

There was no time to ask questions – there was only time to survive. Tom pushed Storm into the welcoming coolness of the wooden cave. Silver ran in afterwards, pressing himself comfortingly against Storm's legs.

"We have to hope this redwood can withstand the flames," Tom said.

"My uncle once told me that redwood trees never burn," Elenna said. "Something in their bark resists fire. The animals will be safe there."

"So will you," said Tom, giving Elenna a gentle push.

Elenna glared at him. "I'm not hiding from anything!" she said.

Tom knew that an argument with

Elenna was one battle he'd never win! She was stubborn as a mule. They soothed the animals one more time, then Tom and Elenna backed out of the safety of the tree, and turned to face the Beast.

The rolling ball of fire was approaching with terrible speed, scorching a path of flame in its wake as it crashed into the clearing where Tom and Elenna stood. The heat was so fierce that Tom could feel the hairs on his arms crisping. Tom had to shield his eyes with one hand to look into the bright flames.

The Beast stopped dead. It began to change shape, lengthening and drawing upwards into a column of pure flame. Two fiery arms pushed out from the central burning pillar, uncurling and sprouting long fingers that ended in claws made of black, curling smoke. Golden flames sparked and snapped about its head. Two cruel red eyes flickered to life. The Beast gazed at them with its terrible, molten face. It gave a mocking bow of introduction.

Dimly, beneath the flames, Tom saw the shadow of a body – black and shrunken. Tom sensed words amid the fierce crackle and spit of fire. The red jewel embedded in Tom's belt shone brightly, the Beast's name creeping into his mind as if the Beast itself was talking to him.

Hellion.

Tom adjusted his grip on the strange, heavy sword, then thrust it at the Beast. There was a nasty crackling sound. It sounded like the Beast was laughing at him.

"While there's blood in my veins, I'll send you home, Hellion!" Tom shouted.

The Beast lashed out. An ancient oak tree in the path of its fiery arm burst into flame as easily as if it was paper. Elenna gave a choking cry and stepped closer to Tom.

Behind them, Storm whinnied from his hiding place. Hellion's glowing eyes widened with interest.

"I'm glad they're safe in the redwood," Elenna said.

The Beast stretched itself to an impossible height, arching a thin arm over Tom and Elenna's heads towards the redwood. Tom twisted round, readying himself. Once the Beast realised the redwood was impervious to its touch, it would likely be more angry than ever.

But, to Tom's horror, a bright line of flame sliced into the bark – the redwood caught alight! Storm whinnied in terror and Silver let out a desperate howl.

Elenna sank slowly to her knees, shaking her head. "No... No... They'll be burnt alive. No... Not again!"

"This isn't your village, Elenna!" Tom shouted, trying to keep her focussed. "They can escape – look!"

Elenna raised her head. As the redwood's trunk blazed in a coat of pure golden flame, the stallion and the wolf raced for their lives across the forest floor.

The Beast started after them. Tom wielded his sword as best he could. He had to distract Hellion, before he burnt Storm and Silver to cinders.

The Beast was shrinking, bringing

its long fiery arms back into its
body, preparing to roll itself into
a fireball again.

Tom thrust his sword desperately
into the flames. His move confused
the Beast, making it uncurl again.
But almost at once, the hilt became
too hot to handle.

Tom tossed the blade across to his
left hand, and thrust again, agonising
pains shooting up his arm. He
wrapped his right hand deep in
his sleeve and took the smoking
sword back.

Tom's sword burnt through his
sleeve almost at once. As it bit cruelly
into the skin beneath, he was forced
to drop the smoking blade. It fell to
the ground with a thud. The grass
beneath it blackened and curled as
Tom stumbled back.

This is impossible! he thought in utter despair.

The Beast stood like a ghastly tree of fire, roaring his displeasure at Tom's attempts to fight him. Elenna started firing arrows at Hellion, but the wooden shafts sizzled to ash before they even touched whatever body lay at the core of the fire.

"We have to think of something else!" Tom shouted.

He suddenly remembered the injured stag, and the way that Hellion's eyes had lit up at the sight of Storm and Silver hiding in the redwood tree. Perhaps there was a way to defeat this monster.

Could they – dare they – use Storm and Silver as bait?

CHAPTER SIX

THE CHASE

Tom hastily explained his plan to
Elenna, who listened carefully.

"Hellion's taking his anger out on
all the living creatures he can find in
the forest," he said, taking up his
borrowed sword from where it had
fallen. The metal was still hot to
touch, but no longer burnt him.
"If we use Storm and Silver, we could
lure Hellion towards the lake over

there. We might be able to douse his flames. And then we'll see what he's really made of!"

Hellion took a step towards them. A burning branch fell from way above, only just missing their heads as Tom dragged Elenna backwards.

"Good plan," said Elenna, brushing off a stray ember that had caught on her clothes.

Tom whistled, praying the animals would overcome their terror and return to the clearing. Hellion roared again, crashing one hand against a beech tree. It fell with a noise like thunder.

Storm and Silver came uncertainly into the clearing, their ears flicking. They had heard Tom's call. As Hellion began lumbering towards the animals, Elenna vaulted into

Storm's saddle. The stallion surged forward, Elenna wrenching his reins to the right to drag him away from the burning Beast. Tom sheathed his sword and ran swiftly after Elenna and the stallion, with Silver loping by his side.

There was a roar of anger behind them. Tom glanced back. Hellion was beating the ground with his fiery fists, like a blacksmith striking an

anvil. Sparks flew in all directions
and the air around him was a
shimmering blur. Tom felt a surge of
sympathy amid his fear – just like the
stag, Hellion was driven senseless
with rage and confusion over
something he couldn't control.
But determination chased away
Tom's pity.

He would send Hellion home.

Tom ran, feeling the ground shake beneath his feet. Hellion was giving chase. A jet of flame shot through the trees, causing branches to catch fire directly over Tom's head. Burning embers floated down, singeing

everything they touched. Tom's clothes were still damp, so the embers did little more than sizzle and steam as they touched the wet cloth of his tunic. But Silver's coat was dry, and soon became dappled with black scorchmarks. The wolf ran steadily beside Tom, ignoring the embers as they burnt through his thick fur. His fierce gaze was trained on Elenna and Storm up ahead.

The air was growing clearer as they left the fire behind. Tom could see a break in the trees. They were nearly out of the forest. He prayed they would see the lake as soon as they burst out of the wood. He knew it would not be long before Hellion caught them. But he only had a rough idea of which way they were running.

Sunlight slashed across Tom's eyes as, at last, he stumbled free of the forest. Hellion's roars of rage weren't far behind. The black water of the lake glittered before them, with its fringe of pale sand. Elenna had dismounted, and she and Storm were both pacing anxiously by the lake shore.

"How are we going to get Hellion into the water?" Elenna asked as Tom ran towards her, panting and out of breath. "He'll never just throw himself in!"

Tom twisted round to look at the forest again. The air above the trees was glowing. Hellion was getting closer. A jet of fire shot out of the canopy as a tall tree went up like a beacon. Overhead, the great black portal pulsed and quivered in the strange glassy dome of the sky. In desperation, Tom turned back to the lake and scanned the shore.

"There!" he gasped, pointing at a rickety jetty some distance away. "I'll lure him onto that, and then escape by jumping into the water."

Tom looked back to see more flames shooting out from the very edge of the forest itself. Hellion was nearly upon them. They could see his outline blazing a trail through the trees. Tom wouldn't be able to reach the jetty in time – unless...

"I need Storm," Tom said.

Elenna looked alarmed. "You'll risk his life?" she gasped.

Tom hoped it wouldn't come to that. He seized Storm's bridle and leapt into the saddle. Storm neighed and tossed his head as Tom pulled the reins hard.

"What are you going to do?"
Elenna asked.

"Survive," Tom said grimly. He
pointed to a cluster of boulders
nearby, just a few paces back from
the edge of the water. "Take Silver
and hide behind those rocks," he
said. "Hellion mustn't be distracted
from chasing me."

He knew Storm could swim. But
would Storm be able to swim all the
way back to the shore once they
jumped off the jetty?

There was only one way to find
out. And as Hellion burst out of the
forest in a blaze of flame and fury,
Tom turned Storm's head and began
to gallop for his life.

CHAPTER SEVEN

INTO THE WATER

Sand sprayed up from beneath Storm's hooves as Tom thundered down the lake shore, his head bent close to the stallion's neck. The lake glistened away to his right. It wasn't far to the jetty. But with Hellion so close, there wasn't much time.

There was a hideous roar. Tom twisted round to see the fiery Beast with his arms held aloft. Even from a distance, Hellion was so bright it was hard to look at him. The Beast stopped briefly, glaring up at the angry portal above. *He wants to go home*, Tom realised.

The Beast roared in frustration and swung left and right, igniting the shrubs and saplings that grew on the edge of the forest. Tom hoped Hellion had not seen Silver or Elenna, who had only just made it to the rocks. He stood up in the saddle.

"Over here!" he shouted, and waved his arms. "Hellion! Come and get me!"

The Beast's flaming eyes sparked and smouldered. He lifted his arm. A great fireball shot from his fingertips. It hit the ground, exploding on impact. Splinters of charred wood exploded. Storm snorted and reared.

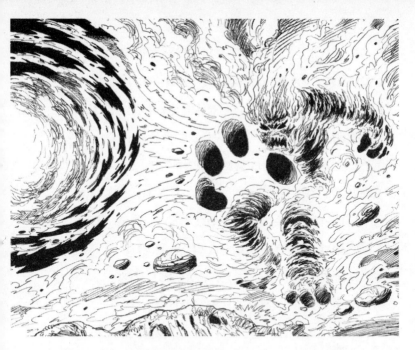

Tom had to squeeze his legs against
the stallion's flanks to stay in
the saddle.

He dug in his heels with all his
might. "Go, Storm!"

Storm took off, straight into the
path of a fireball. Tom swerved
feeling the heat of the fireball as it
shot past and landed harmlessly in
the lake. They were almost there.
Tom tugged Storm's bridle, guiding

him. At Tom's urging, the stallion found a new burst of speed and leapt onto the jetty.

Storm landed awkwardly, staggering – then pulled himself up straight. Snorting and blowing, Tom's faithful friend gazed down the length of the jetty. Hellion was striding along the shore after them.

"We can do it," Tom urged him. "Trust me, old friend."

Storm's ears pricked. Tom tapped his sides lightly with his heels. The stallion began to walk.

The jetty groaned under the weight of Storm's hooves as Tom guided him slowly onwards. It seemed sound, though one or two of the planks had rotted through. Tom knew this could work to his advantage – if they could get Hellion onto the jetty, he might set fire to the ancient timbers and send himself plunging into the lake. It was a big gamble, but Tom had run out of other ideas.

There was another terrible screech behind them. Tom tore his eyes from the narrow, slippery jetty to steal a glimpse of the Beast. Hellion was prowling along the lake shore, clearly wary of the water. For a moment, Tom's eyes locked on the Beast's fiery gaze.

Have I made a terrible mistake coming out over the water this way? Tom wondered. *Have I been too reckless?*

He caught sight of Elenna as she looked over the top of the boulder. She gave him a firm thumbs-up. Even from this distance, Tom could see that she was wearing a grim smile.

He turned back to concentrate on keeping Storm steady on the rotten wood. "Keep going, boy," he said. "A little faster, now."

Storm broke into a cautious trot, his hooves rattling the planks over the water. Tom glanced back. Hellion stood at the shore-end of the jetty. He towered taller than three men.

Tom kicked Storm onwards. There was no turning back now. The red

jewel pulsed in his belt, telling Tom how uncertain Hellion was feeling. Tom felt a thrill of hope ripple through him. He and Storm would make this work.

Then there was no more jetty left. Only the black, glinting water. It was deep out here. Deeper than Tom had thought.

"Well done," Tom whispered, and patted Storm's neck as the stallion

slowed to a stop.

He guided Storm around, taking care not to step too close to the edge of the jetty. They were now facing Hellion.

With a furious bellow, the Beast leapt onto the jetty. Tom felt the planks shake beneath Storm as Hellion raced towards them, the creature's flaming outline burning brighter than ever.

Over Hellion's shoulder, Tom could see what the Beast could not: flaming footprints, burning and smouldering on the wooden jetty. With a crack, the first plank gave way and fell into the lake with a hiss. Then another.

Hearing the sound, the Beast swung back, clearly hesitant. More of the jetty's timbers were burning. Although he was closer to Tom than the shore now, the Beast tried to retreat, but his molten feet burnt through the planks like a hot knife slicing through butter.

Tom pulled out his sword and held it high in the air. The sun flashed on the tip of his blade. "I'm right here!" he challenged the Beast. "It's your move now!"

Through the red jewel, Tom felt Hellion's rage as the Beast lunged forwards. The sudden movement caused the burning pier to collapse to one side. The planks groaned and tipped, splintering and snapping, flames leaping high. Hellion's flickering face pulsed with confusion and panic. He stumbled, wheeling his arms.

Got him! thought Tom.

Letting out an appalling screech,

Hellion toppled into the lake. A huge plume of steam whirled above the black water as the Beast disappeared beneath the surface.

The jetty was badly damaged. More planks fell into the lake, their burning edges hissing and spitting as they touched the water, tendrils of smoke climbing into the sky. Tom felt the entire structure wobble and crumple. Storm whinnied and staggered. It was their turn now...

Tom hit the cold water and fought to twist his body away from Storm's thrashing hooves as everything around him went dark. He tried to find which way was up but, when he opened his eyes, all he saw were waterweeds and drifting planks of wood floating in front of his face.

Pushing them all clear, Tom tried to

settle himself against the panic in his chest, which felt banded with steel. He couldn't take a breath. Not yet...

A bubble trickled from his mouth and drifted away.

Bubbles drift upwards! Tom realised.

He kicked out in the same direction, and saw the blurry sun wavering through the water above his head. He pumped his arms and legs, breaking through the surface and spitting water to take a grateful breath.

Hellion was flailing towards the shore. The Beast's outline had changed beyond recognition. He was still huge, but his body was thin and dark, his arms mere wet stumps at his sides. Tom saw that the Beast was defenceless without his fiery skin; he was no longer invincible.

As hope leapt in Tom's breast, he glanced around for Storm. The stallion was several lengths away, trying and failing to keep his head above the surface.

I should have taken off his saddle! Tom thought, furious with himself. *It's dragging him down.*

Tom struck out towards his horse.

"Hold on, Storm!" he shouted.

He seized Storm's bridle. Storm snorted at him in terror. Together, they sank beneath the lake surface.

Tom kicked, determined not to let go of his horse. But it was no good. They were sinking, deeper and deeper, past the remains of an old fishing boat, tangled nets, weeds waving gently.

Tom's head was bursting, his vision full of stars. He and Storm spiralled

gently through the black water.
Tom's lungs felt as though they
were on fire.

Dimly, he knew that he and Storm
would die here.

The Quest had defeated him!

CHAPTER EIGHT
DOUSED

He felt Storm's head pushing him. His arms floated out to the sides. Light was glimmering over his head, where there had been no light before. They were moving upwards.

Strength surged back into Tom. He kicked hard, still holding Storm's reins, digging deep for strength he shouldn't have had. The water broke over their heads. A breeze rippled over Tom's wet skin and he gulped at the sweet air. He tried to strike out for shore, but his arms were too weak. He felt Storm rising up beneath him, until he was draped across the saddle. Storm swam steadily, strongly, kicking with all his might. The saddle had already pulled Storm down once – but Tom's loyal friend was refusing to give in.

Tom felt a jolt as the stallion's hooves found the muddy lake bed and began to wade to the shore.

"Tom!" Elenna pulled him from the saddle with gasp of joy as Silver raced up and down the shoreline, howling in delight. "I thought you'd drowned!"

Tom fell to the sandy ground, retching and gulping. "So...did I!" he gasped, heaving himself to his feet. "Thanks, friend," he said throwing his arm around Storm's wet and gleaming shoulder. "You saved both our lives."

Storm's answering neigh was lost in a deep roar of defiance coming from the edge of the forest. Tom whirled around. He had forgotten about Hellion!

The Beast stood at the edge of the

forest, snatching up twigs and leaves with his pitifully shortened arms, holding them to his body in an attempt to reignite his flames. It was no good. Everything Hellion touched fizzed and steamed, but nothing sparked.

"He's finished!" Elenna said.

But Elenna had spoken too soon. Snarling with fury, Hellion sent a fireball, smaller than before but no less deadly, hurtling towards them. Tom ducked just in time, pushing Elenna out of the way.

Storm screamed in shock as the fireball collided with his neck. A horrible smell of burning hair rose into the air.

Rage surged through Tom as he noticed part of Storm's mane had shrivelled away to nothing, revealing

bare skin. The Beast could do what it liked to him – but not to the animals!

Tom ran straight for the Beast, reaching for his borrowed sword. But all his hand found was air. The sheath was empty. He realised with a shock that his sword must have sunk into the lake. Thinking on his feet, Tom snatched up a fallen forked branch to use as a makeshift weapon.

Hellion seemed surprised at Tom's move. The Beast stood still, uncertain which way to turn as Tom bore down on him. With a hard thrust, Tom drove the branch either side of Hellion's neck. The Beast howled with pain as he staggered and tripped onto his back. He clutched at the branch that had pinned him to the ground. One arm shot out and directed a weak jet of flame. Tom dodged sideways, losing his grip on the wood, and the flame fizzled, pale and harmless against his wet clothes.

The Beast clambered up weakly and backed away rubbing his neck, but Tom knew he was still powerful enough to destroy him if he stepped too close. How was he going to bring the Beast under control?

His perfect memory drew him a picture of an old fisherman's net, tangled in the remains of a fishing boat. He had seen it while in the lake. If he could find the net, they could cast it over Hellion and pin him to the ground.

Hellion tugged the thorny branch from his stomach and cast it to the ground with another scream of pain and defiance as Tom turned and ran back towards the water.

"I need something from the lake," Tom shouted in answer to Elenna's confused look. "Distract him!"

As he ran, Tom heard the whistling sound of three arrows being fired. Hellion's cries of confused rage tore the air.

Tom took a deep breath and jumped into the lake. He and Storm had been struggling a little way off from the shore. Judging the depth of the water by the blackness as he gazed downwards, Tom dived. His hands found waterweeds, but nothing more. Undeterred, he swam on. More weeds. *The net is here somewhere,* he told himself.

At last, his hands closed on slimy, knotted rope. He tugged hard. The net refused to move. Wrapping part of the net around his hands, he braced his legs against the remains of the old fishing boat and pulled as hard as he could. With a muffled sound, the boat broke in half and the net came free. Tom kicked for the surface and swam back to the shore as fast as he could, the rope heavy and slimy over his shoulder.

Hellion was lurching from side to

side, roaring helplessly as Silver danced about his ankles and Elenna showered the ground with arrows.

"Get back!" Tom panted to them.

Silver backed off at once and Elenna lowered her bow. Tom ran forward. With a huge effort, he lifted the net over his head and whirled it in the air before the Beast realised what was happening. Storm whinnied as the net sailed over the bedraggled monster's head.

Hellion fell with a grunt of surprise. The heavy, wet rope doused the pale flames that had begun to flicker back to life over the Beast's body. Elenna rushed to gather stones heavy enough to weigh the net down around the edges. Hellion roared, but in vain.

The Beast was trapped.

Tom collapsed to the ground. Every
part of him ached. His clothes were
wet. His hands were sore, burnt and
blistered from grappling with both a
burning sword hilt and an unwieldy

net. Every breath he drew was
an effort.

"Well done, Tom," said Elenna
gently. "You can rest now."

Tom shook his head as he got

wearily to his feet. "Not yet, Elenna," he said. "We have to send him back to his home."

He wiped the lake water from his eyes and gazed down at the Beast. Hellion's fiery eyes were dull pinpoints of light. The red jewel in Tom's belt pulsed dully – the Beast knew he was defeated.

On his last Quest, Tom had learnt that the only way to free these Tavanian Beasts was to refuse to kill them, even when they were at his mercy. He held Hellion's gaze for a brief moment. Then he knelt down and loosened the edges of the net.

The flames flared briefly in Hellion's eyes. Elenna flinched, expecting the Beast to lash out. Tom held out his hand to calm her. That flash had offered them gratitude.

With a sigh like a great, fiery wind, Hellion closed his eyes. His great head sank to his chest.

It was over.

CHAPTER NINE

ONWARDS

The clouds rumbled overhead.
Tearing his gaze from the Beast, Tom
looked up into the strange sky. It was
gathering itself up like someone was
crumpling it in a giant fist. Eerie
lights streaked from one side to
the other.

"The portal is pushing the sky
apart!" Elenna gasped.

The black rip in the surface of the

sky was bending and stretching like it was yawning. The sky wrinkled and bent. And then the net snapped back, torn from the ground by an immense force.

Tom and Elenna staggered backwards as Hellion was snatched up. He rose, whirling like a tornado, towards the portal. The portal opened its dark mouth even wider, squeezing apart the clouds on either side. The sky was shot with colour. Elenna gasped and Tom shielded his eyes as Hellion disappeared into the portal. His limbs shone with fire once more. His head wore a crown of flames. Hellion had returned to his full fiery glory.

He was going home.

The great Beast threw out his arms and roared in gratitude. With a thunderous sound, the portal snapped shut. The clouds vanished. Suddenly the sky was clear and blue again – as if the portal had never been there.

Tom and Elenna stood in silence for a moment, their animals quiet by their sides.

Elenna let out a sigh. "We did it," she said.

Tom gave a tired smile. "We saved another Beast."

As Elenna applied a poultice to Storm's wounds, a fleeting dark shape caught Tom's eye. He looked up – from where the portal had been, a curious object was floating to the ground, landing at Tom's feet.

Silver smelt the object cautiously. Tom ruffled the wolf's fur, and bent down to pick it up.

"It's some sort of hat," he told Elenna, studying it. It was made of stiff black linen, decorated with glittering pieces of jet and amber and lined with black satin.

"It must belong to Oradu," Elenna guessed. "Like the cloak we found after we sent Convol home."

Storm thrust his velvet nose into the hat as Tom turned it round in his hands. Something rustled, tucked deep inside the lining. Tom saw a little pocket, sewn near the rim. He pulled out a sachet of dried, sweet-smelling herbs.

"Bay leaves," Tom said, peering inside. "Lavender too, I think, and shavings of what looks like rosewood. And these little black specks are dried bilberries."

"Ingredients," Elenna murmured.

"One of Oradu's potions, I expect. I wonder what kind of potion could be made with them?"

Tom slipped the sachet back into its hiding place. As he did so, the hat sailed out of his hands and hovered before him. At the same time, the wizard's cloak slipped out of Storm's

saddle and floated beneath the hat, as if draped around an invisible pair of shoulders.

A gust of wind pulled the floating specks of ash out of the air and moulded them into a shape below the hat that filled out the cloak. The grey outline of a figure emerged as they watched.

"Oradu!" Tom said.

The Good Wizard of Tavania was coming back to strength as his possessions were reunited.

Elenna and Tom watched as golden light sparked in the air before the vision. The fizzing light formed itself into a long, looping line. Tom could make out a word, shaking and shimmering with magic.

Krestor.

Tom looked wordlessly at Elenna.

Krestor? Was this the name of the next Beast they were to face?

The golden light disappeared, leaving only a faint outline of the word Krestor in the air. Tom gathered the cloak and hat together and placed them back into the saddle bag. This time, he wasn't surprised when both items shrank in order to fit the leather pouch.

Tom was tired and hungry. He knew Elenna and the animals felt the same. This Quest was taking every ounce of their strength and courage. He climbed slowly into Storm's saddle. Beneath the glassy orb of Tavania's sky, now clear and unblemished above the Forest of Doom, they set off.

"Look, Tom," said Elenna, laying her hand on his arm.

Tom saw the injured stag which had attacked him earlier. The great beast was panting, limping slowly away from the smouldering remains of the forest. He followed its gaze to a group of does and fawns grazing on a patch of open grass on the horizon.

The stag stumbled and almost fell. Elenna gasped in sorrow at the sight of such a mighty animal in distress. Tom forced himself to watch as the stag limped onwards, then broke into a painful run.

Tom knew the creature was proud and determined. He would reach his family if it was the last thing he did. Tom felt a glimmer of hope to see such courage in the face of so much disaster.

Whatever Malvel was doing to Tavania, it had to stop. The suffering had to end. And Tom knew that he was the only person who could make this happen.

Wondering about the strange, uncertain future, Tom clicked his tongue and tapped Storm gently with his heels. Elenna glanced up at him and smiled reassuringly. The four companions moved on down the winding road. They would see this through together – whatever it took.

Here's a sneak preview of Tom's next exciting adventure!

Meet

KRESTOR
THE CRUSHING
TERROR

Only Tom can save Tavania from the rule of the Evil Wizard Malvel...

PROLOGUE

Aquillus spread his wings as a swell of warm air lifted him higher.

He soared over a mountain range, but tiredness flooded through him. He'd been hunting for far longer than he wanted and still had no food to show for it. He thought of his chicks, their beaks open with hunger. They would starve if he did not feed them soon. Aquillus couldn't go on like this. He needed rest.

The eagle spotted a sun-bleached tree, clinging to the mountainside where he could rest. He swooped downwards.

Aquillus landed on the uppermost branch of the tree and folded his wings. Tavania's mountains reared up in front of him, unforgiving and proud. The small streams that used to flow between white rocks were dry.

The branch beneath Aquillus shuddered in a stiff breeze. The eagle clung on with his yellow talons, then opened his wings and slowly rose into the air. He may not have been able to find water, but maybe he could find food. An unwary mountain rodent, perhaps, out searching for something to drink...

His sharp eyes searched the mountains but he saw no creatures darting between the rocky crevices.

Aquillus could almost hear the urgent squawk of his chicks. He'd left them for too long. Failure seemed to weigh him down as he angled himself in the direction of his nest.

Follow this Quest to the end in KRESTOR THE CRUSHING TERROR.

Win an exclusive
Beast Quest T-shirt and goody bag!

Tom has battled many fearsome Beasts and we want to know which one is your favourite! Send us a drawing or painting of your favourite Beast and tell us in 30 words why you think it's the best.

Each month we will select **three** winners to receive a Beast Quest T-shirt and goody bag!

Send your entry on a postcard to
BEAST QUEST COMPETITION
Orchard Books, 338 Euston Road, London NW1 3BH.

Australian readers should email:
childrens.books@hachette.com.au

New Zealand readers should write to:
Beast Quest Competition, 4 Whetu Place, Mairangi Bay,
Auckland NZ, or email: childrensbooks@hachette.co.nz

**Don't forget to include your name and address.
Only one entry per child.**

Good luck!

Join the Quest,
Join the Tribe

www.beastquest.co.uk

Have you checked out the Beast Quest website?
It's the place to go for games, downloads, activities,
sneak previews and lots of fun!

You can read all about your favourite Beasts, download free screensavers and desktop wallpapers for
your computer, and even challenge your friends
to a Beast Tournament.

Sign up to the newsletter at www.beastquest.co.uk
to receive exclusive extra content and the opportunity to enter special members-only competitions.
We'll send you up-to-date info on all the Beast
Quest books, including the next exciting series
which features six brand-new Beasts!

Get 30% off all Beast Quest Books at www.beastquest.co.uk
Enter the code BEAST at the checkout.

Offer valid in UK and ROI, offer expires December 2013

All books priced at £4.99.
Special bumper editions priced at £5.99.

Orchard Books are available from all good bookshops, or can
be ordered from our website: www.orchardbooks.co.uk,
or telephone 01235 827702, or fax 01235 8227703.

FREE COLLECTOR CARDS INSIDE!

Series 7: THE LOST WORLD
COLLECT THEM ALL!

Can Tom save the chaotic land of Tavania from dark Wizard Malvel's evil plans?

978 1 40830 729 8

978 1 40830 730 4

978 1 40830 731 1

978 1 40830 732 8

978 1 40830 733 5

978 1 40830 734 2

FREE COLLECTOR CARDS INSIDE!

Series 8: THE PIRATE KING OUT NOW!

Sanpao the Pirate King wants to steal the sacred Tree of Being. Can Tom scupper his plans?

978 1 40831 310 7

978 1 40831 311 4

978 1 40831 312 1

978 1 40831 313 8

978 1 40831 314 5

978 1 40831 315 2

DARE YOU DIVE INTO

SEA QUEST

FREE COLLECTOR CARDS INSIDE!

SERIES 1
COLLECT THEM ALL!

Deep in the water
lurks a new breed of Beast!

978 1 40831 848 5   978 1 40831 849 2   978 1 40831 850 8   978 1 40831 851 5

www.seaquestbooks.co.uk